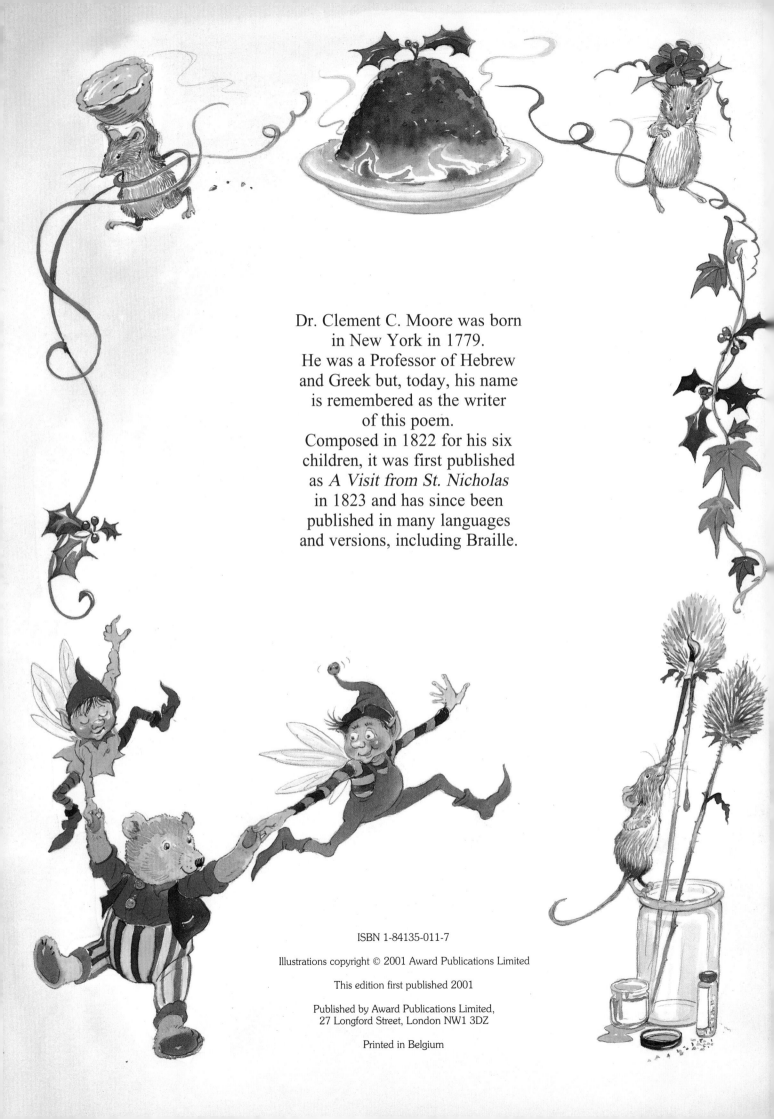

Dr. Clement C. Moore was born
in New York in 1779.
He was a Professor of Hebrew
and Greek but, today, his name
is remembered as the writer
of this poem.
Composed in 1822 for his six
children, it was first published
as *A Visit from St. Nicholas*
in 1823 and has since been
published in many languages
and versions, including Braille.

ISBN 1-84135-011-7

Illustrations copyright © 2001 Award Publications Limited

This edition first published 2001

Published by Award Publications Limited,
27 Longford Street, London NW1 3DZ

Printed in Belgium

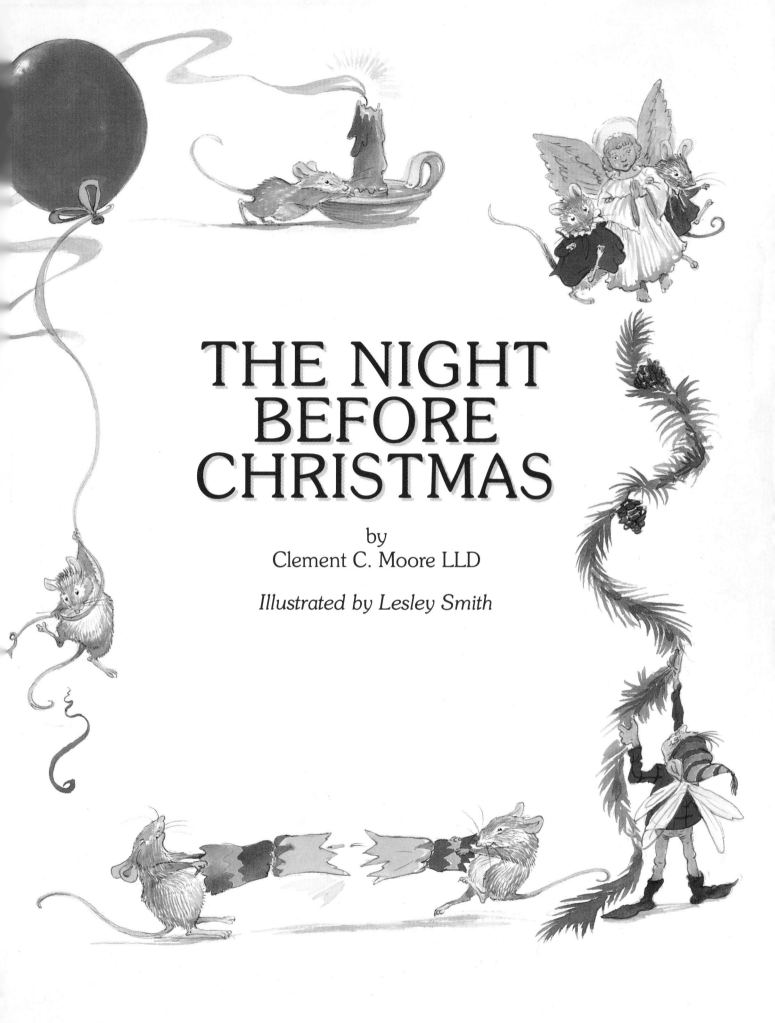

THE NIGHT BEFORE CHRISTMAS

by
Clement C. Moore LLD

Illustrated by Lesley Smith

AWARD PUBLICATIONS LIMITED

'Twas the night before Christmas,
    when all through the house
Not a creature was stirring,
    not even a mouse;
The stockings were hung by
    the chimney with care,
In hopes that St Nicholas
    soon would be there;

The children were nestled
all snug in their beds,
While visions of sugar-plums
danced in their heads;

And Mamma in her kerchief,
  and I in my cap,
Had just settled our brains
  for a long winter's nap;

When out on the lawn
there arose such a clatter,
I sprang from the bed
to see what was the matter.

Away to the window
I flew like a flash,
Tore open the shutters
and threw up the sash.

The moon on the breast
of the new-fallen snow,
Gave lustre of midday
to objects below.

When what to my wondering
    eyes should appear,
But a miniature sleigh and
    eight tiny reindeer,
With a little old driver,
    so lively and quick,
I knew in a moment
    it must be St Nick.

More rapid than eagles
   his coursers they came,
And he whistled and shouted,
   and called them by name:
"Now, Dasher! now, Dancer!
   now, Prancer and Vixen!
On, Comet! on, Cupid!
   on, Donner and Blitzen!

"To the top of the porch,
    to the top of the wall!
Now dash away! dash away!
    dash away all!"
As dry leaves that before
    the wild hurricane fly,
When they meet with an obstacle,
    mount to the sky,
So up to the housetop
    the coursers they flew,
With the sleigh full of toys,
    and St Nicholas too.

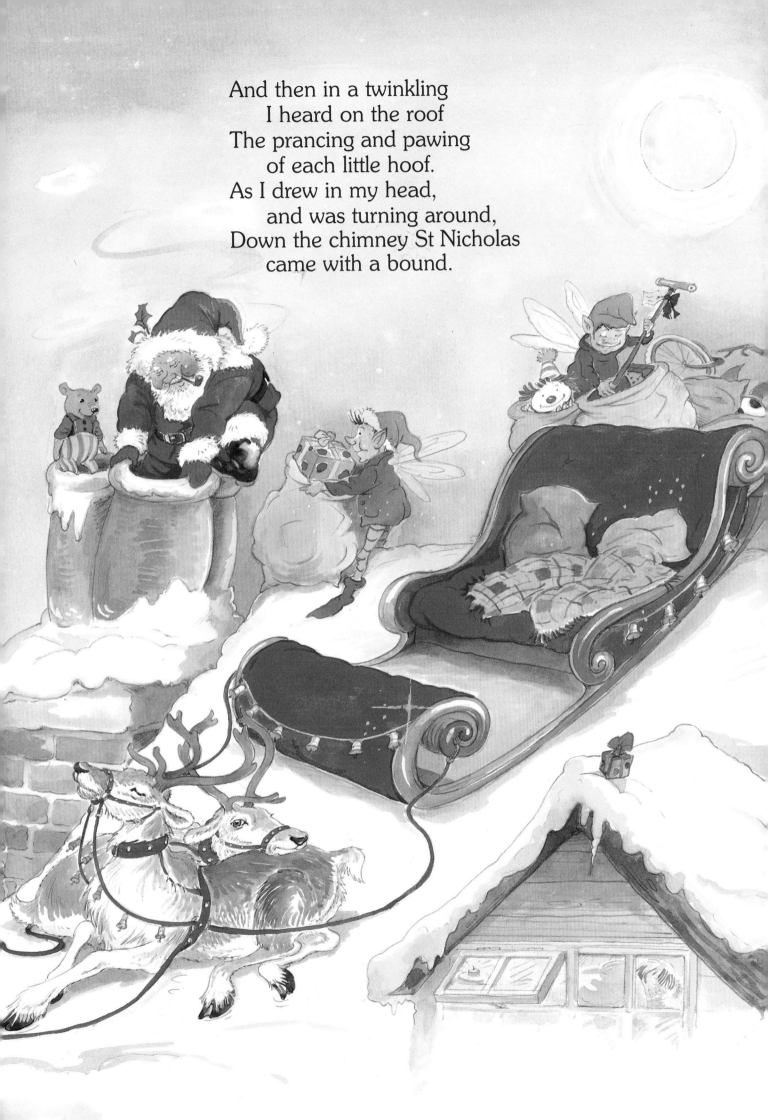

And then in a twinkling
        I heard on the roof
The prancing and pawing
        of each little hoof.
As I drew in my head,
        and was turning around,
Down the chimney St Nicholas
        came with a bound.

He was dressed all in fur
    from his head to his foot,
And his clothes were all tarnished
    with ashes and soot;

A bundle of toys he had
   flung on his back,
And he looked like a pedlar
   just opening his pack.

His eyes – how they twinkled!
    his dimples, how merry!
His cheeks were like roses,
    his nose like a cherry!
His droll little mouth
    was drawn up like a bow,
And the beard on his chin
    was as white as the snow.
The stump of a pipe
    he held tight in his teeth,
And the smoke it encircled
    his head like a wreath.

He had a broad face
    and a little round belly,
That shook, when he laughed,
    like a bowl full of jelly.
He was chubby and plump,
    a right jolly old elf;
And I laughed when I saw him,
    in spite of myself.

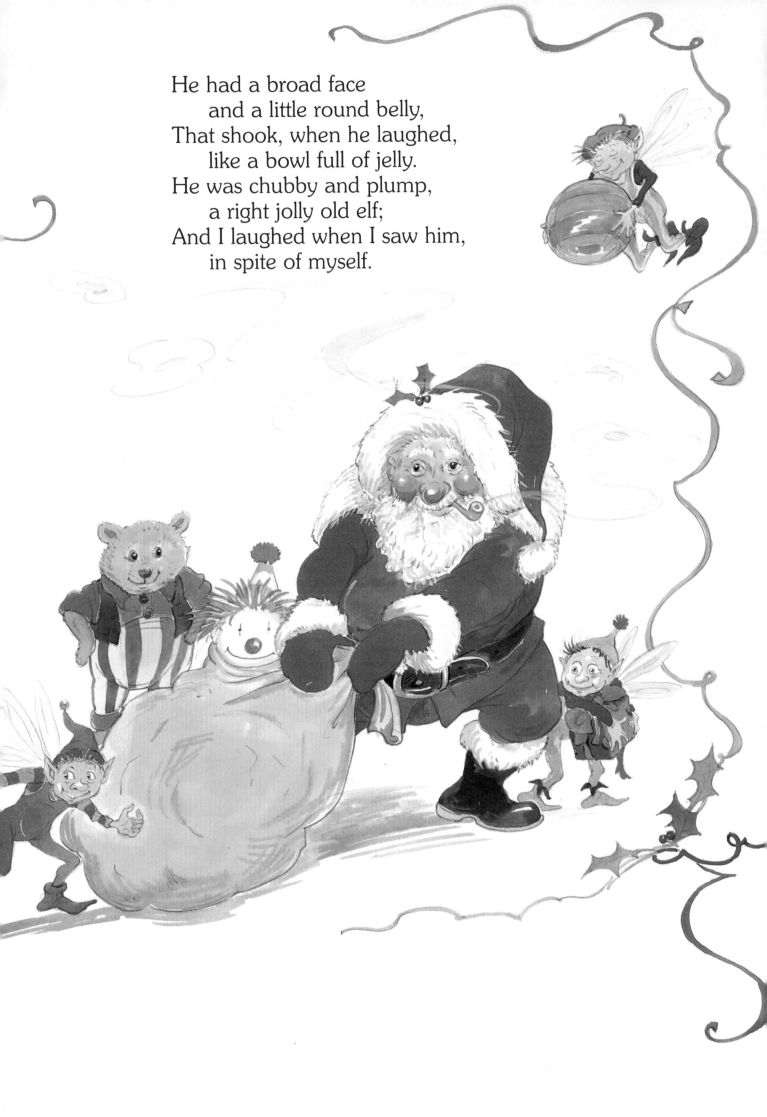

A wink of his eye and a
   twist of his head
Soon gave me to know
   I had nothing to dread.

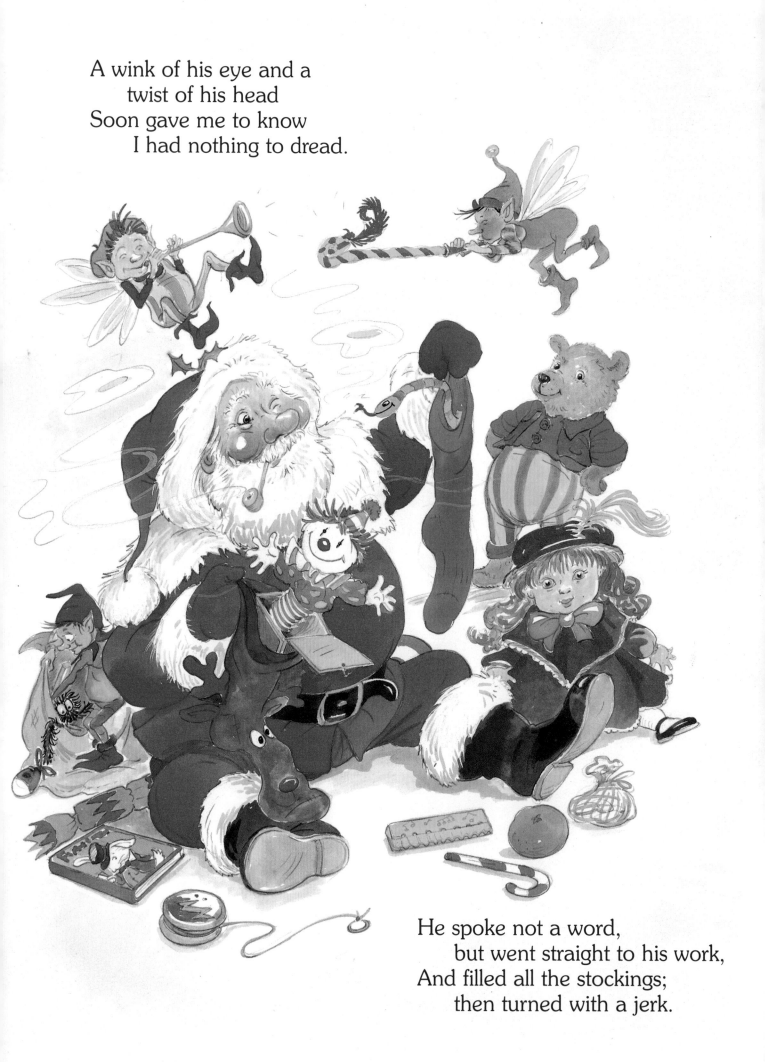

He spoke not a word,
   but went straight to his work,
And filled all the stockings;
   then turned with a jerk.

And laying his finger aside
    of his nose,
And giving a nod, up the
    chimney he rose.

He sprang to his sleigh,
   to his team gave a whistle,
And away they all flew
   like the down of a thistle;

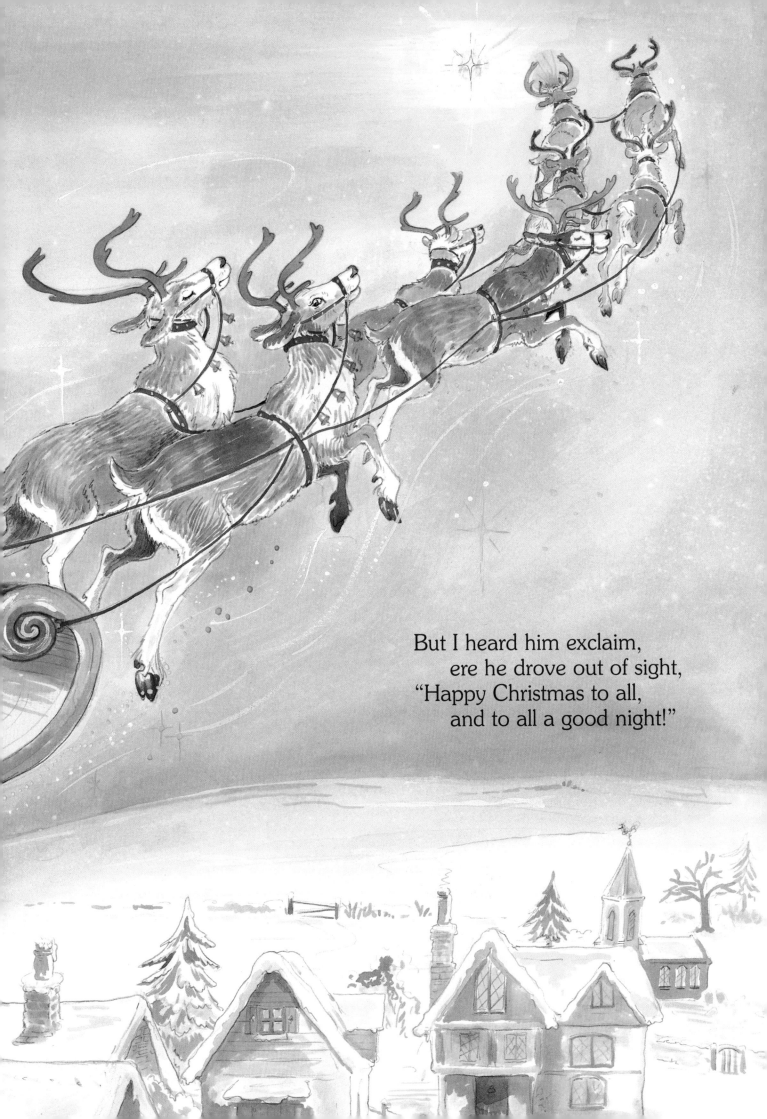

But I heard him exclaim,
ere he drove out of sight,
"Happy Christmas to all,
and to all a good night!"